Bright ■Summaries.com

The disappearance of Stephanie Mailer

by Joël Dicker

BOOK ANALYSIS

Written by Morgane Fleurot
Translated by Oliver Brown

The disappearance of Stephanie Mailer

BY JOËL DICKER

JOËL DICKER

SWISS WRITER

- **Born in 1985 in Geneva**

- **Some of his works:**

  - *The Last Days of Our Fathers* (2010), novel

  - *The Truth About Harry Quebert* (2012), novel

  - *The Baltimore Book* (2015), novel

Joël Dicker is a young author on the rise. Initially a graduate of the University of Geneva in law and formerly a parliamentary attaché in Switzerland. He now devotes himself to his passion: writing. His second novel, *The Truth About Harry Quebert* (2012), which won the Goncourt Prize for high school students, has sold 5 million copies and has been translated into 40 languages. After a first historical novel (his characters are secret agents of the SOE), the writer wanted to try his hand at writing an American-style thriller.

Published by De Fallois since his very first book (2010), Joël Dicker has paid tribute to his publisher (who died on 2 January 2018) in this latest novel, *The Disappearance of Stephanie Mailer.*

THE DISAPPEARANCE OF STEPHANIE MAILER

A GIGOGNE COLD-CASE

- **Genre:** crime novel

- **Reference edition:** *La disparition de Stephanie Mailer*, Paris, Éditions de Fallois, 2018, 640 p.

- **1ʳᵉ edition:** 2018

- **Themes:** thriller, disappearance, murder, suspense, New York suburbs, investigation, theatre, mystery novel

The Disappearance of Stephanie Mailer is a dense novel with the feel of an American thriller. Joël Dicker returns to the success of his second book, *The Truth About Harry Quebert*, and sets his action in the United States, a few hours from New York in the Hamptons. But this time, it is not Nola Kellergan who has disappeared, but Stephanie Mailer, a distinguished journalist who was investigating a twenty-year-old case involving a theatre festival and a quadruple murder. Although the reviews are mixed, Joël Dicker nevertheless repeats the feat of an effective *page-turner*.

SUMMARY

1993-1994

Orphea, a small town in the Hamptons, about 100 kilometres from New York, is under the thumb of its mayor, Joseph Gordon. He enforces the law by taking bribes from the inhabitants as soon as they require the town hall's approval for their activities. As usual, Gordon tries to bribe Ted Tennenbaum, a young man with an imposing build and a fighting spirit, but the latter stands up to him: he has plans to build his restaurant, the Athena Café, and intends not to give in to the mayor's blackmail.

At the same time, Ted Tennenbaum is in trouble with the kingpin Jeremiah Fold, a pimp and drug dealer whom he has severely beaten and humiliated, and who has since blackmailed him by threatening to burn down his restaurant and house. Jeremiah has taken to recruiting his mules, known as his "minions", by means of an original if unorthodox method: prostituting the beautiful Mylla, an underage girl, and blackmailing her clients. But everyone's ordeal is cut short when Jeremiah dies tragically in a violent road accident in 1994.

Meghan Padalin is a young bookseller living in Orphea. When she hears about the blackmailing by the town hall, she threatens Gordon orally every night and reports him to the deputy mayor, Alan Brown, by making an anonymous call to him. She is also involved in an extramarital love affair with the critic Meta Ostrovsky, who is madly in love with her.

30 JULY 1994

On the opening night of the first Orphea Festival, a quadruple shooting takes place: that of the Gordon family (the mayor, his wife and their son) and of Meghan Padalin, who was an inconvenient witness to the scene.

Ted Tennenbaum is quickly suspected by the police: his van was seen in front of the mayor's house at the time of the murders; the whole town knows about his differences with Gordon, and above all, the police know for a fact that he is in possession of a Berreta pistol which would be the murder weapon.

Detective Jesse Rosenberg and Sergeant Derek Scott are put in charge of the investigation and manage to gather substantial evidence leading to Tennenbaum's arrest. Tennenbaum is then caught and killed in a car chase with the police, during which Jesse's fiancée Natasha is also killed. After the death of the main suspect, the case is closed.

2013-2014

Policewoman Anna Kanner divorces her husband and moves from New York City to the suburbs, to the quiet town of Orphea. She is brought into the precinct as the deputy chief of police, as Mayor Brown has promised her the chief's job once he retires.

At the same time, in New York, the young Dakota Eden is implicated in a case of moral harassment having pushed to suicide Tara, one of her classmates. Dakota allegedly retaliated after Tara deleted a valuable file from her computer: the play she had been writing for a whole year.

Steven Bergdorf, the editor of the *New York Review of Letters*, is in a passionate love affair with Alice Filmore, his employee. She is unconsciously trying to ruin him with her costly demands, while Steven tries to hide the affair from his wife.

SUMMER 2014 BEFORE THE FIRST

As he prepares to take early retirement, Jesse Rosenberg is approached by a young journalist who tells him her name is Stephanie Mailer and that she has been looking into the 1994 quadruple murder case. She tells him that she has new information. According to her, the culprit is not Ted Tennenbaum. Following the mysterious disappearance of Stephanie, Jesse decides to reopen the 1994 investigation and calls Derek, his partner of the time. They will also be assisted by Anna, the only police officer in the Orphea police station who is intrigued by the case. When the body of the missing journalist is found drowned, the three heroes are reinforced in their certainty. Twenty years later, the 1994 murderer is still at large and fears being discovered.

When they try to get their hands on the police report of the time, they find that it has disappeared: where should it have been? A single piece of paper with the enigmatic words "THE BLACK NIGHT". This dark night refers to a play written by Kirk Harvey, chief of police of Orphea at the time of the events of 1994. When questioned, Harvey is mysterious and promises to reveal the name of the culprit if his play is performed at the twentieth theatre festival a few days later. Mayor Brown grants his request and Kirk auditions his actors. He chooses Jerry and Dakota Eden, the father and his depressed daughter who are passing through Orphea; Steven Bergdorf (the former editor of the local newspaper *The Orphea Chronicle*) and his mistress Alice; Gulliver, the current chief of police; Samuel Padalin, Meghan's widower; and finally Ostrovsky, the famous critic. He also recruits Charlotte Brown, the mayor's wife, who is quickly questioned because she was seen driving Tennenbaum's van on the night of the murder by a new witness. She is later cleared but remains a suspect. Michael Bird, the editor of *the Orphea chronicles*, is assigned to cover the event from the inside and attends all the rehearsals, which are kept secret. When Dakota is shot as her character is about to reveal the name of the 1994 perpetrator, all the actors are under suspicion. Kirk Harvey then reveals that he had no idea who the culprit was and was hoping that he would come forward during the performance.

SUMMER 2014 AFTER THE FIRST

By analysing the position of Meghan Padalin's body, Anna, Jesse and Derek discover that she was in fact the intended victim in 1994, and that the mayor and his family were only unfortunate witnesses to the scene. They retrieve Meghan's diaries from her husband's possession, and when they read them, the investigation takes an important step forward. There was not one, but two murderers who had switched. Mayor Gordon wanted to murder Meghan Padalin because she was a threat to his corrupt business, so he let someone else do it while he took care of Jeremiah Fold. So we have to find out who wanted Jeremiah dead in order to catch the killer of Meghan, the mayor, and Stephanie Mailer.

Anna, because she recognised her in a photograph, manages to unmask Mylla, Jeremiah's former prostitute who, following the death of her tormentor, has taken on her true identity and is now married to Michael Bird. Michael, Jeremiah's former 'stooge', was madly in love with Mylla. He, therefore, planned to assassinate their torturer and allied himself with Ted Tennenbaum who also wanted to get rid of the blackmailer. It is Ted who has the idea of the exchange with mayor Gordon and who sets up an ingenious stratagem. He is the only one to know who are the two murderers and entrusts them with the names of the victims by means of a coded message in two books from the bookshop. Understanding that he is a suspect, Michael tries to get rid of Anna, who is close to the end, but she is saved *in extremis* by Jesse and Derek. The culprit eventually confesses to the 1994 and 2014 murders.

CHARACTER STUDY

THE POLICE TEAM

Jesse Rosenberg

The main hero of the story, Jesse is a captain in the New York State Police and is about to retire at the beginning of the novel, when he is only 45 years old. Brilliant by his colleagues' admission, he is also handsome. Despite his undeniable strengths, Jesse is haunted by the death of his fiancée Natasha, a death that seems to be linked to the 1994 case. It is certainly this reason that pushes him to reopen this case twenty years later, even though it has been solved.

Derek Scott

Derek Scott is Jesse's former teammate in the field. He retired after the 1994 case and still works for the State Police, but in the administrative department where he is bored stiff. Married to Darla and with a family, he does not hesitate to reopen the 1994 investigation, even though it may upset his family.

Anna Kanner

After her divorce, Anna moved to Orphea where she serves as the second deputy chief of the Orphea Police Department. Previously a negotiator for the New York

State Police, she left her position after accidentally kill-
ing a hostage. She is the only woman in the Orphea
police station and as such is first admired and then
rejected by her colleagues. Visibly very attractive, it is
repeatedly stated that Anna magnetically catches the
eye as she passes. Immediately alerted by Stephanie
Mailer's disappearance, she completes the team formed
by Jesse and Derek to investigate the 1994 case. Her
help will prove invaluable. Being conscientious, the
young woman likes to surprise by her efficiency.

Ron Gulliver

Gulliver is the chief of police of Orphea and Anna's
superior. He has a large body and an unbalanced diet.
He is naturally vulgar and unpleasant. He is also reluc-
tant to participate in the investigation. Moreover, he is
only interested in himself, since he resigns (p. 429) during the investigation in order to take part in Kirk
Harvey's play at the theatre festival.

Jasper Mountain

Jasper Montagne is the deputy chief of the Orphea
police, as is Anna, and he fears that his colleague will
beat him to the post of new chief of police. His ice-cold
physique (in keeping with his surname) is matched
only by his bad fate. In this, he resembles Chief Gulliver,
of whom he seems the 'worthy' successor.

Major McKenna

The Major is Jesse and Derek's direct boss in the State Police. His impulsive temperament suggests a military career. Although stern and uncompromising, he seems to take a liking to the team and regularly gives them extra time to complete the investigation.

Kirk Harvey

Kirk Harvey was the head of the Orphea police force at the time of the 1994 quadruple murder; he left town in a hurry shortly after the case. Twenty years later, he is a "lunatic" (p. 351) who lives in Los Angeles and tells anyone who will listen, including aspiring actors, that he is writing "the play of the century. At the request of Mayor Brown, he returns to Orphea to help solve the investigation, but more importantly to finally bring his masterpiece to the stage. He is an extravagant character who contributes to the comic relief of the novel. He can also be a liar and duplicitous.

THE PEOPLE OF ORPHEA

Charlotte Brown

Formerly Kirk Harvey's girlfriend and once an actress, Charlotte was the lead in the play *Uncle Vanya* which opened the first Orphea Theatre Festival. Beautiful and smiling, she is now the wife of Mayor Brown and works in a veterinary clinic. She is quickly drawn into the investigation, as she was absent from the theatre minutes before the performance at the time of the 1994 murder.

Alan Brown

As the town's mayor, Alan Brown soon becomes involved in the investigation and makes frequent appearances in the novel. He is characterised in particular by his marked animosity towards Captain Rosenberg, against whom he lashes out. He was deputy mayor at the time of the 1994 affair and was prematurely removed from his position, although there is evidence that he was involved in the organised escape of Mayor Gordon, prevented by his murder.

Michael Bird

Michael is the editor of the *Orphea chronicle*, the city's daily newspaper. He succeeded Steven Bergdorf as editor of the paper when Bergdorf left the paper shortly after the 1994 murders. He was also Stephanie Mailer's last employer. He shows great willingness during the investigation and even lends his premises to the police team when they no longer feel safe at the police station.

Miranda Bird

The difference in age between them is significant; she is several years younger than him. Her past is discreetly exhumed by the police when they discover that she was used as bait by Jeremiah Fold to recruit his stooges.

In the end, she proves to be completely unaware of her husband's past and present actions.

Cody Illinois

A neighbour and friend of Anna's, he was the first to show her affection when she arrived in the city. He is a bookseller by trade and, before his murder, when the investigation was reopened in 2014, is a valuable supporter and witness to the stories and mores of the town in 1994. He was already running the bookshop at that time and had Meghan Padalin as an employee.

THE VICTIMS

Meghan Padalin

The first character to appear in the novel, Meghan is initially seen as a collateral victim of the 1994 murder, an inconvenient witness to be eliminated. It turns out that she was the main target.

Stephanie Mailer

The eponymous character, Stephanie, makes only a brief appearance at the beginning of the story when she comes to New York and arouses Jesse's curiosity by revealing to him that she had detected a mistake in their 1994 investigation. First employed at the *New York Review of Letters*, she then works at the *Orphea chronicle* before being found drowned near Orphea. This last element confirmed to the police the need to reopen the 1994 case.

Joseph Gordon

Murdered in Orphea in 1994 along with his entire family, Gordon was then the town's mayor. During the 2014 investigation, the police discover his involvement in corruption cases that would give a solid motive to many of the town's residents. He is in fact a collateral victim, an unfortunate witness to the murder of Meghan Padalin.

Natasha Darrinski

Natasha was Jesse's fiancée and an accomplished cook on the verge of realizing her dream of opening her own restaurant. Tragically, she died during the police pursuit of Ted Tennenbaum (the number one suspect in the 1994 investigation).

THE NEW YORK REVIEW OF LETTERS

Steven Bergdorf

The editor of the *New York Letters* magazine is a coward, a hypocrite and a weakling. He is caught up in an infernal love spiral with his young mistress Alice. He only takes her to Orphea with the original intention of murdering her to get rid of her. But he keeps changing his mind and reveals an unstable character. This situation makes him an ideal culprit for the 1994 murders. He is violent, inconsistent, clumsy and quickly overwhelmed by events.

Alice Filmore

Capricious, full of herself; convinced that she is an author in the making, her intentions with Steven Bergdorf are unclear. She says she loves him but seems to be using him more as a means of obtaining material possessions, or as a means of professional advancement since she thinks he is capable of elevating her manuscript to bestseller status.

Meta Ostrovski

A critic by trade, Ostrovsky has been employed by the *Revue* for several years. He is extremely full of himself and his position, to the point of caricature. Nevertheless, his unconditional love for Meghan Padalin makes him an endearing character. He is also the sponsor of Stephanie's book.

THE EDEN FAMILY

Dakota Eden

Dakota is a notoriously depressed 19-year-old whose life is crumbling on drugs. A born playwright, she hasn't written since she drove a fellow student to suicide a year ago.

Jerry Eden

Jerry, a multi-millionaire, is the managing director of the famous Channel 14 television station and incidentally Dakota's father. To save his daughter from being shipwrecked, he decides to take her to Orphea to recharge during the events of the story.

Tara Scalini

Tara is Dakota's childhood friend and had fallen in love with her as a teenager. Humiliated by Dakota after confessing her love, she is eventually found hanging in her room.

KEYS TO READING

A NEST OF NOVELS

Multiplication of viewpoints

Formally, *The Disappearance of Stephanie Mailer* is a novel with drawers, i.e. the main story is embellished with embedded side stories that constitute as many retrospectives as different narratives. In fact, if we look at the way the novel is divided up, a certain mechanism can be seen: each new chapter is overlaid with the name of the protagonist who lends his or her point of view to the story that follows. In order to clarify the narrative as much as possible, three narrator characters are recurrent: Jesse, Derek and Anna. Jesse's point of view is the most represented, which contributes to making him the hero of the novel. Moreover, each of his chapters carries an additional piece of information: a countdown to the first day of the festival.

But it is also possible to follow the first-person narratives of Steven, Jerry, Dakota and Meghan. However, the structure remains clear, the points of view echo each other and some of them provide answers to questions previously asked by other characters: for example, Dakota's chapter (p. 436) proposes to follow up on Jerry's chapter and reveal why "everything has changed" (p. 332).

Multiple retrospectives

Where Jesse tells the story in the first person, that of the 2014 investigation, Anna and Derek's narratives are anchored in a specific space-time: Derek recalls the 1994 investigation with Jesse, while Anna recounts her life in New York and her move to Orphea between 2010 and 2014. Embedded in these first-person excerpts are also third-person retrospectives that look back at a specific point in time, most often experienced by protagonists who are now deceased. However, each narrative seems to tend towards one and the same point of sublimation, which is suggested by the countdown of the chapters (-7, -6, -5, etc.): '0 The evening of the first' (p. 469). Indeed, it is at this point that the climaxes of Jesse, Anna and Derek's three main narratives come together, each engaged with the following: 'Saturday 26 July 2014 [...] The day everything turned upside down." (p. 471), 'Friday 21 September 2012. The day it all fell apart." (p. 479), "Thursday 13 October 1994. The day everything changed" (p. 483).

This multiplication of narrative strings gives the novel a fast and lively rhythm that is enhanced by numerous dialogues, to give it an increasingly cinematographic and multiform dimension. Indeed, these memories occurring just after a dialogue with a witness, or after a piece of information that a character has kept quiet because of his or her embarrassment, have all the makings of Hollywood *flashbacks*.

A REFLECTION ON WRITING

Multiform writing

The novel, in its script-like guise, produces several genres that intersect and intertwine. We will distinguish three distinct genres because they have formal writing requirements: the novel, of course, but also the theatre and the diary. The latter is represented in particular by the excerpts from Meghan Padalin's diary (pp. 558-560), which add dynamism to the writing and the narrative. However, the exercise is interesting because these extracts, although written in the first person, do not use the same enunciative devices as Anna's narratives for example. The latter is read as if Anna were addressing them to an ignorant reader: they take the time to explain, to detail, to contextualise, in short, to narrate. In contrast, Meghan's diaries are delivered as they are, entirely introspective as if to project the reader into the role of the investigator. They do not bother with explanations and remain self-centred, as shown by the opening statement of the diaries: "Happy New Year to me. (p. 558).

As for the theatre, it is very present: it can be read, and seen and constitutes a set of which the novel itself is the stage. This is why the story opens with a description of the setting up of Orphea's new event, which "that evening [...] inaugurated its very first theatre festival" (p. 9), like a didascalia contextualising the scene of the drama to come. To corroborate this idea, it is interesting to note that the De Fallois publishing house has provided a "List of Main Characters", which can be consulted on page 637, and which is reminiscent of this obligatory mention in every edition of theatre. Kirk Harvey's play thus enters the narrative as a play within a play and introduces a whole vocabulary and dramatic universe that reinforces this theme. Finally, the play *Uncle Vanya* is frequently cited (as it was the first play produced at the 1994 festival) and is intended to serve as a literary reference to the author or as a tribute.

 UNCLE VANYA

Chekhov's *Uncle Vanya*, written in 1897, was more successful than the playwright had originally anticipated. The play features characters who are worn out by life, mostly disillusioned, and who miss each other and the potential happiness that could result from their encounters. *Uncle Vanya* is a rewrite of another Chekhov play written in 1890: **The Man in the Woods**, which was originally a comedy, and which was very badly received by the critics: its transformation dramatised it considerably.

The writing of the book in abyss

This phenomenon of interpenetration between the written book appearing in the read book is a theme already developed by Joel Dicker. In *The Truth About Harry Quebert*, his hero (Marcus Goldman) is a writer looking for inspiration for his second novel; he ends up writing the adventure he is living. Here, our heroes discover that

'Stephanie was devoting an entire book to the case' (p. 114), which she entitled 'Not Guilty'; what's more, it is 'excitingly written' (p. 115).

The mysterious sponsor of Stephanie's book (we learn later that it is the critic Meta Ostrovsky), promises her to write a 'wonderful detective story' (p. 115) which readers 'will enjoy' (p. 115): so many glowing reviews for the novel we have in our hands, which has the same plot! Moreover, the character of the critic is interesting; his functions are very often analysed and contrasted with 'the minor art' (p. 133) of writing. Ostrovsky declares himself the 'police of intellectual truth' (p. 133). Joel Dicker caricatures this profession by denouncing the arbitrary practices of his character, who writes murderous reviews without even having opened the books (p. 135). When Ostrovsky becomes an actor in the play, he undergoes a kind of metamorphosis and gains humility, as if the author, like Kirk's revenge against Ostrovsky (he ridicules him in his play), had also taken revenge on the image of the critic.

THE SPRINGS OF COMEDY

Comedy of character

Meta Ostrovsky, through this transformation, becomes a comic theatre character, yet he already had the seeds of this state within him. When he is invested in the role of a critic, he is nothing but exaggeration and caricature, 'an important man' (p. 133) or *God, but for the better* (p. 136) are his own words to define himself. The frequent use of free indirect discourse (page 132 and page 133) contributes to making him a detestable, but comical character. Moreover, his presence is always noticed, as evidenced by his efforts to do so; he does not speak, but 'bawls' (p. 133), 'yells' (p. 337) or even 'shrieks like a damned man with a too high voice' (p. 338).

Like him, Gulliver 'bawls' (p. 337) and makes a fool of himself during performances where he holds a 'stuffed wolverine' (p. 398), wearing pants, and performs a stage roll that we can easily imagine being 'pitiful' (p. 398) given the appearance of the chief of police, whose stoutness is matched only by his silliness. As his down-to-earth response to Anna's riddle ('I want to write, but I can't write. Who am I?" (p. 334): "Answer: A penguin" (p. 335).

Comedy of words and gestures

As for Kirk Harvey, he is intrinsically a theatrical character; his mechanics are based on oral and body language, and he is made up of nothing but grandiloquence and gesticulations. This is evidenced by his first performance entitled *I, Kirk Harvey*, in which he considers himself capable of being both director, author and actor of a monologous play in which he is the sole protagonist. This dissonance between his ambitions, his self-esteem and the impressions he makes on those around him creates a notorious discrepancy, and this discrepancy is an incubator of comedy. What is more, the nouns that characterise him as 'crazy' (p. 269), 'a walking joke' (p. 316) or even 'an old fool' by his own admission (p. 350) contribute to a colourful and buffoonish picture. Kirk's own thoughts reflect his penchant for exaggeration and emphasis: when he inwardly gloats, "Oh dear glory, so long coveted, here you are at last" (p. 338), we can note the use of the exclamation mark (which most often punctuates his sentences) or the lyrical "oh", characteristic of the poetic or tragic parody here.

These characters also constitute an entry into comedy via their lexical usage. Kirk, for example, does not hesitate to call his detractors and other opponents flowery names: insults such as "Poison!", "Batracian!" or "gastric bile" (p. 262) add a burlesque dimension to the dialogue. Interjections such as "Bigre" (p. 212) and "Pfft!" (p. 213) are also at odds with the usually smooth narration. The transformation of the name 'Rosenberg' into 'Leonberg' (p. 213) serves as a comparison between the policeman and the huge, clumsy-looking dog whose breed bears that name.

SYMBOLIC BORROWING

Orphea and the descent into hell

This burlesque superstrate, anchored in the concrete, coexists with a symbolic substratum touching on the metaphysical, notably through names and the superimposition of a mythological universe in the world of detective fiction. "Orphea", to begin with, does not deny its link with Orpheus, whose myth is one of the most poignant in ancient Greece. Moreover, Ted Tennenbaum seems to be aware of this parallel, as he names his café

Athena, in reference to the Greek goddess of war and knowledge. And even though the narrative does not dwell on this point, it is not a coincidence; the Greek affiliation is well-claimed since Ted's van bears the owl, the goddess's fetish bird, a detail that will lose him.

This mythological echo is corroborated by the 'Sphinx of Thebes-like' (p. 334) riddle that Anna writes on the magnetic board when the investigators question the identity of the mysterious sponsor of Stephanie's book: 'I want to write, but I can't write. Who am I?" (p. 334).

 THE OEDIPUS MYTH

The figure of the Sphinx, a winged creature with the body of a lioness and the head of a woman, is part of the myth of Oedipus, the tragic hero condemned to kill his father and marry his mother. Arriving at the gates of Thebes, Oedipus finds himself confronted with the monster that terrorises the city, devouring anyone who fails to solve its riddles. Here is the one he proposes to Oedipus: "What is the animal that in the morning has four legs, at noon two, and in the evening three, and that is all the more slow and vulnerable because it has no legs?"

The answer to this famous riddle is 'man', who crawls on all fours as a child, stands on two legs as an adult and, as he grows older, uses a cane to walk. The Sphinx, defeated by Oedipus, rushes off a cliff and the hero enters Thebes now free of the creature.

Biblical resonances and medieval beliefs

Moreover, if 'mail' designates the action of sending, 'mailer' would be a substantival form meaning 'messenger', this parallel linking Stephanie to the figure of the god Hermes. The messenger is a recurring figure in mythology and also finds resonance in the Catholic religion, where prophets and apostles are the guarantors of the word of God. And this divine word is that of Stephanie, who has come to tell Jesse a "truth" (p. 19) in the present tense of general truth: "You haven't solved this case, Captain. (p. 19). The journalist will be murdered. Like her, most often in the Bible, the messengers are misunderstood visionaries destined to end up as martyrs. Among them, we note "Jeremiah", the name of one of the 1994 victims, which echoes the previous thesis. Finally, before Tara's suicide, the Eden family is living happily in the "Garden of Eden" (p. 436), the name of their summer residence. This play on words implies both their own surname and a biblical reference to the wonderful garden of Genesis. But any Garden of Eden suggests guilt and then fall: Tara driven to suicide by Dakota, then Dakota's slow descent into hell.

Hell is embodied in the play *La Nuit noire*, written by Kirk Harvey, whose very title is tinged with apocalyptic symbolism. The former police chief uses this dimension to promote the play in 1993 and 1994: he writes apocalyptic messages on the walls ('*The Dark Night will soon begin*' [p. 162]) and thus creates a real rumour of the end of the world, which is whispered fearfully by all the inhabitants of Orphea. What is more, when Alice lets a journalist into the rehearsal room, she warns him by correcting him: this is not a 'theatre door', it is 'the door to Hell' (p. 451). Finally, the Latin text spoken by Meta Ostrovski in the play (*'Dies irae, dies illa,//solvet saeclum in favilla!'* is taken from a medieval poem of apocalyptic inspiration. For the last symbolic references are echoes of the Middle Ages; to take just one example, the character of Kirk assumes the role of the medieval madman: respected because he is the bearer of truth.

AVENUES FOR REFLECTION

A FEW QUESTIONS FOR FURTHER REFLECTION...

- The novel has the peculiarity of starting in chapter 7. Explain this feature and its relevance to the construction of the story.

- On page 270, a detail already gives us a glimpse of who the real victim of 30 July 1994 is.

- How does Kirk Harvey promote his play for the first Orphea Theatre Festival? What is the key to understanding this?

- The lexical field of theatre is found throughout the novel; find eight terms relating to this universe.

- Apart from the diary and the theatre, what other forms of writing does the novel stage?

- Look at the passage from page 489 to 499. What types of comedy are set up in this chapter and which characters are the vectors?

- What country is Natasha from? What are the different elements that make it possible to affirm this?

- In your opinion, what is the point of having characters like Dakota and Jerry in a detective story?

TO GO FURTHER

REFERENCE EDITION

La disparition de Stephanie Mailer, Paris, Éditions de Fallois, 2018.

BENCHMARK STUDIES

Atlas de la mythologie, Paris, Éditions Glénat, 2003.

KOUTCHOUMOFF L., "Joël Dicker, Genevan, 27 years old, dreamed of writing a great American novel. He did it", in *Le Temps*, 15 September 2012. Accessed on 18 October 2018.

https://www.letemps.ch/culture/joel-dicker-genevois-27-ans-revait-decrire-un-grand-roman-americain

Official website of Joel Dicker, "Biography", in JoelDicker. Accessed 18 October 2018.

https://joeldicker.com/biographie/

Your opinion is important to us!
Leave a comment on the website of your online bookshop
and share your favourites on social networks!